Henry Melville King

# A Summer Visit of Three Rhode Islanders to the Massachusetts Bay in 1651

An account of the visit of Dr. John Clarke, Obadiah Holmes and John

Crandall, members of the Baptist Church in Newport, R. I.

Henry Melville King

**A Summer Visit of Three Rhode Islanders to the Massachusetts Bay in 1651**
*An account of the visit of Dr. John Clarke, Obadiah Holmes and John Crandall,*
*members of the Baptist Church in Newport, R. I.*

ISBN/EAN: 9783337381318

Printed in Europe, USA, Canada, Australia, Japan

Cover: Foto ©Andreas Hilbeck / pixelio.de

More available books at **www.hansebooks.com**

# A SUMMER VISIT

OF

# THREE RHODE ISLANDERS

TO THE

# MASSACHUSETTS BAY IN 1651

AN ACCOUNT OF THE VISIT OF DR. JOHN CLARKE,
OBADIAH HOLMES AND JOHN CRANDALL, MEMBERS
OF THE BAPTIST CHURCH IN NEWPORT. R. I., TO
WILLIAM WITTER OF SWAMPSCOTT, MASS., IN JULY,
1651 : ITS INNOCENT PURPOSE AND ITS PAINFUL
CONSEQUENCES

BY

## HENRY MELVILLE KING

PASTOR OF THE FIRST BAPTIST CHURCH, PROVIDENCE, R. I.

PROVIDENC

## PRESTON AND ROUNDS

1896

# PREFACE

THE substance of this paper was presented at the midwinter meeting of the Backus Historical Society, held in Boston, Dec. 8, 1879. It was published (Boston, 1880), by vote of the Society, under the general title—"Early Baptists Defended, a Review of Dr. Henry M. Dexter's Account of the Visit to William Witter in 'As to Roger Williams.'" It has been quoted frequently as an authority in reference to the historical incident which it discusses. Dr. Dexter found a copy of it in the Library of the British Museum. For several years it has been out of print, and the demand for it, on the part of the increasing number of students of colonial history, could not be met.

The history of the visit has been carefully re-examined, and the paper has been considerably lengthened by the addition of new

1*

matter, and made to include a consideration
of the incident as symptomatic of the Puritan
spirit, and as shedding light upon the cause
of the banishment of Roger Williams — a
question which a few writers and speakers
are not willing to allow to remain settled.
The recent discovery of incontrovertible doc-
umentary evidence will confirm the belief
that has been generally held as to the religious nature of Williams' offence, and ought
to be able to remove all doubts from all
minds.

This paper was read, in its enlarged form,
before the Rhode Island Historical Society
at its meeting, March 5, 1895, and before the
Veteran Citizens Historical Association of
Providence, April 11, 1895.

# A Summer Visit

## OF THREE RHODE ISLANDERS TO THE MASSACHUSETTS BAY IN 1651.

The memorable visit of Dr. John Clarke, Obadiah Holmes and John Crandall, members of the Baptist church in Newport, to William Witter, one of the early settlers in the Massachusetts Bay, took place in July, 1651. It is proposed in this paper to review the history of that visit, that we may ascertain, if possible, the object of it, the alleged criminal conduct of which these troublesome visitors were guilty, and the severity of the punishment which they received at the hands of the Puritan magistrates.

This service has been undertaken solely in the interests of historic truth, and not in the spirit of a partizan or a controversialist. A difference of opinion having been manifested of late in high quarters, and views put forward in opposition to those which had been universally held, it seems desirable that there should be a thorough and candid re-examination of the facts in the case which are accessible. When such historians as Dr. J. G. Palfrey ("History of New England") and Dr. H. M. Dexter ("As to Roger Williams") who follows Dr. Palfrey closely and even outstrips him in the positiveness of his convictions, call in question accepted opinions in matters of colonial history, it is due that those opinions be reviewed in the light of all the evidence, old and new, that can be presented.

A high regard for the many sterling

qualities of our Puritan ancestors, and admiration and gratitude for the noble service which they rendered, and the inestimable benefits of which we are enjoying, make us desirous to judge them fairly in all things, and even charitably where they were undoubtedly in error. We certainly would not misjudge their spirit or their acts, and if any false judgments have come down to us, transmitted through ignorance or prejudice, it is high time they were abandoned. On the other hand, a sacred regard for the truth of history should keep us from any disposition to conceal the errors of the Puritans or to extenuate their sins. Great and good as they were, they were not perfect; and he who undertakes to justify all the acts of his fathers, natural or denominational, will find himself burdened with a grave responsibility.

It should be remembered that we are dealing with events nearly two centuries and a half old, when truths now well developed, full grown and generally accepted, were in their infancy and acknowledged by few. We should be careful lest we unconsciously carry back to that early period of our history the standard of to-day, and measure events which occurred then by the fuller wisdom which we now possess. We should be no less careful lest, forgetting the growth and advancement that have been made, we seek to bring past events into closer harmony with present views and wishes than the facts will warrant. The duty of the historian is simply to write history, not to modify it or make it appear different from what it is. The truth may be judged charitably; but the truth is history, and nothing else is.

Let us consider, first, what was the object of the visit which Clarke, Holmes and Crandall, members of the Baptist church in Newport, made to William Witter, a farmer residing in Swampscott, about two miles from Lynn proper. Backus introduces the account of this visit with the following statement ("History of the Baptists," Vol. I., 178): "On July 19, 1651, Messrs. Clarke, Holmes and Crandal, 'being the representatives of the church in Newport, upon the request of William Witter of Lynn arrived there, he being a brother in the church who, by reason of his advanced age, could not undertake so great a journey as to visit the church.'" Backus gives as his authority the Newport church papers, from which the statement is a quotation. Arnold says in similar language ("History of Rhode Island," Vol.

I., 234): "They were deputed by the church to visit an aged member, residing near Lynn, who had requested an interview with some of his brethren." From these statements it appears that the visit was one of Christian sympathy, the pastor and two other members of the church, with its knowledge and consent, making the journey to carry comfort to the heart of an aged and infirm brother, who, as we learn elsewhere ("History of Lynn," by Lewis and Newhall), had already been arrested twice for expressing, in the emphatic language of the times, his opinion against infant baptism, and who, deprived of the privileges of the church and of the sympathy of those whose faith was in accord with his own, had requested this interview. This view has been uniformly accepted as explaining the innocent, humane, religious purpose of the visit. We have no statement from either of the three visitors which sheds any further light on the matter. In the letter of Mr. Holmes to John Spilsbury, William Kiffen and other brethren in London, incorporated by Clarke in his "Ill Newes from New England" (Mass. Hist. Coll., Vol. II., Fourth Series), he says: "I came upon occasion of businesse into the Colony of the Mathatusets, with two other Brethren." If they were deputed by the church to make this visit, this is all the explanation the language requires; this was the "occasion of businesse" which took them to Swampscott.

In opposition to the prevalent view,— a view which seems to be supported by incontrovertible authority,—Dr. Palfrey has suggested that the visit had a very shrewd political purpose, and was care-

fully planned to that end; that owing
to local disagreements in the Providence
Plantations, and the supposed fear of
Clarke and his friends that an attempt
was about to be made to unite Newport
and Portsmouth to the colonial confederacy, or possibly to annex them to the
Massachusetts Bay, it was determined
to prevent such a union; and this method
was deliberately chosen to call forth an
exhibition of the persecuting spirit of the
authorities of the Bay, that the breach
might be widened and the suspected de-
signs of those who were thought to be
laboring for the annexation, might be
frustrated.

It will be necessary to sketch briefly
the situation. William Coddington, who
in 1648 was elected the second President
of the Providence Plantations (though at
that time certain charges were brought

against him, the nature of which is un-
known), had indeed manifested a desire
for a union with the Colonies. There is
much about Coddington's conduct which
is veiled in mystery. He was evidently
a wily, determined, ambitious man. In a
letter of his to Winthrop, under date of
Aug. 5, 1644, a letter which Dr. Palfrey
calls "a curious letter," written, it will
be noticed, five months after the signing
of the charter given to Roger Williams
for the incorporation of the Providence
Plantations, he said: "I desire to have
either such alliance with yourselves or
Plymouth, one or both, as might be safe
for us all, I having chief interest on this
island, it being bought to me and my
friends; and how convenient it might
be, if it were possessed by an enemy,
lying in the heart of the plantations,
and convenient for shipping, I cannot

but see; but I want both counsel and strength to effect what I desire. I desire to hear from you, and that you would bury what I write in deep silence: for what I write I never imparted to any, nor would to you, had I the least doubt of your faithfulness that it should be uttered to my prejudice." The intent of this letter is obvious. It was written about the time the knowledge of the charter to Roger Williams was received in this country, and one month before the second meeting of the Commissioners of the four Colonies. It reveals Coddington's character, and his ambitious purpose. We cannot dwell upon the details of Coddington's conduct. Four years later — in 1648 — in another letter to Winthrop, he disclosed his growing alienation from the people of Providence and Warwick. In September of that year he applied, in connection with Alexander Partridge, to the Commissioners of the Colonies for a union of the Island with them. The application declared that it was endorsed by "the major part of our island"—a statement which was proved false by subsequent events. This application was refused. The Commissioners were unwilling to recognize the island as a distinct colony—the thing which Coddington evidently desired—and offered their protection only on condition that the island should place itself under the government of Plymouth—the thing which Coddington evidently did not desire. That would have defeated his ambitious purpose. He declined the proposition; and here the matter ended. Four months afterward he sailed for England, where he remained at least two years and a half. His design in going to England he succeeded in keeping a profound secret. This is acknowledged by all. The exact time of his return is uncertain. It was probably very soon after the visit to Witter. It could not have been before. When, however, he did return, it was found that he had succeeded, at the very end of his visit, in obtaining a "commission" from the Council of State to institute a separate government over the islands of Rhode Island and Conanicut—thereby setting aside the patent of the Providence Plantations given to Roger Williams, March 14, 1644. This commission appointed Coddington governor for life. He was to be assisted in the government by Councilors, "not exceeding the number of six," who were to be chosen annually, but must be approved by the governor. Having accomplished his ambitious purpose, and procured a division of the Providence Plantations, and the appointment of himself for life as well-nigh the supreme ruler of Newport and Portsmouth, he arrived home possibly in August, 1651.

This act of Coddington is supposed to furnish the probable occasion of the visit of the three Newport worthies to Mr. Witter, in which they found Massachusetts about as hot a place as a fiery furnace heated to a seven-fold temperature.

Dr. Palfrey says: " If Massachusetts was intolerant of Baptists, and if the execution of Coddington's scheme would place the Rhode Island Baptists more or less under her control, the necessity of self-defence admonished them that, if possible, that scheme should be defeated. Clarke had known for seven years that his presence would not be allowed in Massachusetts. During that time a law had existed which his presence would affront. [This was the intolerant law of 1644 banishing all persons who should oppose infant baptism or deny the right of the magistrates to punish the outward breaches of the first table.] And indeed seven years earlier yet, he had gone away under circumstances which made it next to certain that had he not departed voluntarily he would have been expelled.

"Fourteen years he was content to stay away from Massachusetts: in the fifteenth he was prompted to go thither. The considerate reader may see a significance in the time of this movement. The precise day of Coddington's arrival from England with his 'Commission' is not known; but it seems to have been when his arrival was expected from

week to week, or even from day to
day, that Clarke undertook his journey.
Clarke was a man of influence and
authority. His personal character, his
sacred office, and his newly acquired
position of Assistant in the government,
placed him prominently before the people. He was a man of discernment and
resolution, and felt no reluctance to ex-
pose himself to personal inconvenience
for the furtherance of what he accounted
a good public object. And he judged
well that, at this moment, some striking
practical evidence of the hostility of
Massachusetts to Baptists would be effi-
cacious to excite his Rhode Island friends
to oppose the ascendency of Coddington.

"Clarke took with him two companions, one of whom, he could promise
himself, would, at the moment, be almost as unwelcome a visitor as himself.

John Crandall was so far a person of consideration that we find him to have sometimes served in the General Court of the Colony as Commissioner (or Deputy) for Newport. But Obadiah Holmes was a man of more importance. He was minister of the congregation which had occasioned the application from Massachusetts to Plymouth; and he had been recently presented by the Grand Jury of that Colony for a disorderly meeting with others on the Lord's day. The three proceeded together to Lynn, ten miles on the further side of Boston."

Dr. Palfrey continues the narrative with the use of such words and phrases as "perhaps," "it may easily be believed," "as is probable," showing that while he regards his theory as probable he does not present it as a fact capable of proof. It is a conjecture of his own,

for which he offers no authority beyond
what he thinks he finds in the conjunc-
tion of events.

We pause to point out two or three
errors in Dr. Palfrey's narrative. He
says that Clarke left Massachusetts
"under circumstances which made it
next to certain that, had he not departed voluntarily, he would have been
expelled." This language casts an unwarranted reproach upon Clarke and his
conduct, when first in Massachusetts.
He himself says: "In the year '37 I left
my native land, and in the ninth month
of the same, I, through mercy, arrived in
Boston. I was no sooner on shore but
there appeared to me differences among
them touching the Covenants &c." He
goes on to say that "seeing they were
not able so to bear each with other in
their different understandings and con-

sciences, as in those utmost parts of the World to live peaceably together," he himself proposed "for as much as the land was before us and wide enough," to seek out some other place. Very likely had this peace-loving citizen remained in the Bay he would have been banished, even as Roger Williams and a dozen others were; but no reproach should be cast upon the record of "the modest and virtuous Clarke," as Bancroft calls him, "whose whole life was a continued exercise of benevolence," and who "left a name without a spot." Having left the Bay in order to avoid strife, it seems utterly inconsistent that he should return to the Bay in order to stir up strife.

Moreover, Dr. Palfrey has fallen into an error when, in holding up Dr. Clarke's conspicuous character as well calculated

to call forth the religious hostilities of
the authorities of the Bay, he speaks of
"his newly acquired position of Assistant in the government," for according
to the official table given by himself
(*i. e.* Palfrey) Dr. Clarke had been an
Assistant for the two previous years,
but in 1651 did not hold the office; so
that what little force this point seems
to have, falls to the ground utterly.

We now turn to Dr. Dexter's account
of this matter. He shows himself to be
the more than willing disciple of Dr.
Palfrey. He swallows him bodily, conjectures, errors and all, although the
palfrey is hardly less than a moderate-
sized camel. In his dexterous treatment
suppositions become established facts,
and conjectures become accredited history. Having alluded to the remonstrance which the General Court of

3

Massachusetts sent to the General Court of Plymouth in regard to its mild treatment of Holmes, he proceeds:

"Some months before this, William Coddington, sick of the unsettled state of civil affairs, which proved to be the result of the unorganized individualism which was then the key-note of the Rhode Island Plantations . . . . had gone to England to see if something could not be done in the way of remedy. He then obtained leave from the Council of State to institute a separate government for the islands of Rhode Island and Conanicut, he to be Governor, with a Council of not more than six Assistants. In the autumn of 1650 it was understood that he was on his way home with this new instrument; and it was further understood that it was Mr. Coddington's desire and intention

to bring about under it, if possible, the
introduction of Rhode Island into the
Confederacy then existing of the other
Colonies, if not absolutely to procure
its annexation to Massachusetts. . . .
When the crisis approached, Clarke
seems to have felt that a little persecution of the Anabaptists — if such a
thing could be managed — by Massachusetts, might serve an important purpose in prejudicing the Rhode Island
mind against Coddington's scheme.  An
occasion appears accordingly to have
been made, by which the red flag of
the Anabaptistical fanaticism could be
flouted full in the face of the Bay bull."
And so Dr. Dexter continues : " Knowledge of Mr. Witter's case reaching Mr.
Clarke, a pilgrimage was determined
upon for the purpose of public sympathy with this person, if not his open

rebaptism and reception into the Newport fellowship. Such an expedition had in itself a promising look. It would lead through Boston, yet not far enough beyond it to imperil the desired publicity. . . . . The scheme succeeded perfectly," etc.

Dr. Dexter represents the knowledge of Mr. Witter's case as reaching Dr. Clarke just at this crisis, as if it was a happy juncture of events. But he must have been acquainted with it for years, for it had been eight years since Mr. Witter's first arraignment for holding Baptist views, and five years since his second arraignment. Dr. Clarke could not have remained uninformed about it all this time, inasmuch as Witter was a member of the church of which he was pastor. Dr. Dexter attempts to cover up the real character of Mr. Coddington's design by keeping out of sight two points, viz., that he secured in his commission for himself a *life appointment* as Governor, and, secondly, that the election of his Councilors was not valid *unless confirmed by himself*.

But the principal criticism upon this quotation from Dr. Dexter is to be made upon the very remarkable statement that "In the autumn of 1650 it was understood that he (Coddington) was on his way home with this new instrument; and it was further understood that it was Mr. Coddington's desire and intention to bring about under it, if possible, the introduction of Rhode Island into the Confederacy then existing of the other Colonies, if not absolutely to procure its annexation to Massachusetts." It will be noticed that in this theory the question of time is a very important one. Coddington's supposed design and its successful accomplishment must have been understood sufficiently early before the visit to Mr. Witter to allow Dr. Clarke and his companions to mature their plans as to the best course to be pursued. Dr. Dexter, in his anxiety to give time enough, says it was understood that Coddington was on his way home with his Commission " in the autumn of 1650." Now, it so happens that this was at least six months before the Commission was given. Coddington, whose purpose in visiting England, it will be remembered, he had kept a profound secret, must have reached there soon after the execution of Charles I. and the downfall of the British monarchy. The Council of State under the Commonwealth held its first meeting,

Feb. 17, 1649, in the third week after the beheading of the king. Such were the agitations in England, and such the pressure of home business, that two full years elapsed before any attention was given to the Colonies, or, in other words, before Coddington could obtain a hearing. At a meeting of the Council, Feb. 18, 1651, a committee was appointed "to consider of the business of plantations," and six weeks later, April 3, 1651, by a vote of the Council, Coddington received his Commission.

As has been already remarked, the time of Coddington's return to this country is a matter of uncertainty. It was probably soon after the visit to Witter, and is generally put down as in August, 1651. He would have been likely to return as quickly as possible after accomplishing the object of his visit, and may have brought the news of his Commission with him: so that it could not have been understood "in the autumn of 1650" that Coddington was on his way home with his Commission; and no more could it have been understood that "it was his desire and intention" to bring about under it the introduction of Rhode Island into the Confederacy of the Colonies or its annexation to Massachusetts. Setting aside the question of time, which makes strongly against the new theory, Coddington's "desire and intention" must be determined by his previous conduct in declining the annexation, and by the nature of the Commission which he asked for and procured.

In general, then, it may be said against the theory that the visit to Mr. Witter had a political purpose:—

I.   There is not a scintilla of proof
of it, and no authority for it whatever.
It is a specimen of hypothetical history,
with all the known facts squarely against
it.   Dr. Dexter cites Dr. Palfrey, and
Dr. Palfrey cites nobody.

II.   If Coddington's design was such
as this theory supposes, and the defeat
of which is supposed to be the object
of the visit to Mr. Witter, it could not
have been understood by Dr. Clarke
and his companions before their visit
was planned and made.

III.   If Mr. Coddington's design was
such as this theory supposes, there was
no necessity whatever for this visit as
a method of defeating it.   The hostility
of the authorities of the Bay to Baptist
principles, their intolerance and persecuting spirit, were too well known already to require any new exhibition.

The severe law of 1644, condemning to
banishment all persons who "shall either
openly condemn or oppose the baptizing
of infants, or go about secretly to seduce
others from the approbation or use thereof, or shall purposely depart the congregation at the administration of the ordinance, or shall deny the ordinance of
magistracy, or their lawful right or authority to make war, or to punish the
outward breaches of the first table," had
been put on the statute book, and kept
there in spite of the "Petition and Remonstrance" of a few prominent citizens.
Thomas Painter, of Hingham, had been
cruelly whipped for refusing to have his
child baptized. Complaints against such
proceedings had been sent over from
England, and Mr. Winslow had been
commissioned to go to England and answer them. Mr. Witter himself had

been twice arraigned before the Court. Mr. Holmes and two others had been brought to trial at Plymouth, and when they had been treated leniently and bound over, a remonstrance from the Court at Boston had been sent "urging the Plymouth rulers to suppress them speedily." And all this in addition to the treatment which Roger Williams and many others had received. Surely there was no doubt as to the spirit and temper of the Massachusetts Bay, and no occasion for any new demonstration.

Moreover, Mr. Coddington had few friends and sympathizers in Rhode Island in any scheme he might propose. It would have been voted down by an overwhelming majority. His statement, when seeking an alliance with the Colonies in September, 1648, that a major part of the Island desired it, is not sustained by facts which are known. When the character of his Commission was discovered, a request was presented to Dr. Clarke, signed by sixty-five of the inhabitants of Newport and forty-one of the inhabitants of Portsmouth, who, it is said, constituted nearly all the free inhabitants, that he would go to England to secure the rescinding of Mr. Coddington's Commission. Dr. Clarke yielded to this request, and, in connection with Roger Williams, who was sent by Providence and Warwick, made such representations before the Council of State that on October 2, 1653, it voted "to vacate Mr. Coddington's Commission and confirm their former charter."

IV. The facts in the case do not warrant the belief that Mr. Coddington's "desire and intention" in procuring his Commission was to bring Rhode

Island into alliance with the four Colonies, and, much less, under the influence and control of Massachusetts. He had, indeed, three years before, for reasons not fully explained, sought a division of the Providence Plantations and a friendly league with the Confederacy. It is possible that he may have looked upon the league as the only method, at that time, of accomplishing the division on which he seemed bent. When, however, annexation to Plymouth was recommended, he positively declined any such condition of protection. His journey to England was successful. He fully accomplished his object. The result disclosed the full extent of his design, so far as we know. Rhode Island was separated from Providence and Warwick. It became an independent colony, and he was to be its Governor

4

for life, with the powers almost of dictator.

V. There was little ground to fear that Massachusetts and Plymouth would consent to a league with Rhode Island, on account of their unrelenting hostility to the principles and practices of its inhabitants. The application for such a league had been refused again and again. "In truth," it has been said, "these Rhode Island people grew, from the beginning, more and more intolerable to the Boston brethren. It was bad enough that they should obstinately maintain the rights of independent thought and private conscience; it was unpardonable that they should assume to be none the less sincere Christians and good citizens, and should succeed in establishing a government of their own on principles which the Massachusetts General Court declared were criminal. Even in a common peril the Massachusetts magistrates could recognize no tie of old friendship, —hardly indeed of human sympathy,— that should bind them to such men."

VI. Causes quite sufficient are discoverable to account for the opposition to Mr. Coddington. There were religious differences between him and the other leaders, which "grew to such heat of contention that they made a schism among them." Moreover, affairs in England, which were now approaching a crisis, had undoubtedly no little influence on the state of things in the Plantations. Coddington was a royalist,— while Clarke, Nicholas Easton and other leaders were republicans, and the republican party was the dominant one. And still further, there was a very general determination to resist the division of

the Providence Plantations, and to stand
by the original charter. Coddington's
ambitious scheme was enough, in itself,
to arouse the most bitter and determined
opposition.

VII.   If Dr. Clarke and his companions had planned their visit for a political
purpose, viz., to draw forth the intolerant
spirit of the magistrates of the Bay, and
had been so anxious to succeed in it, as
they are represented to have been, it is
perfectly amazing that they did not go
directly to Boston or even to Salem, in
one of which places they would be much
more likely to find the "Bay bull" kept
than in such a quiet, obscure, out-of-the-
way place as Swampscott, which was two
miles even from Lynn.   That this place
should have been the terminus of their
journey is strangely inconsistent with
any such motive as is ascribed to them.

Their supposed shrewdness seems to
have failed them in the most vital point
of their plan.    Having determined to
seek persecution, they took the surest
method to escape it.

VIII.   We are told distinctly by what
ought to be good and sufficient authority that the object of the visit was to
minister Christian sympathy to an aged
brother in the church.    The visit was
made to Swampscott because the brother
whom they came to comfort, lived in
Swampscott.    This statement rests upon
the authority of the Newport Church
Papers, on which Dr. Dexter attempts to
throw discredit, in order to break down
their testimony.    He says : "Backus, indeed, professes to quote (Vol. I., 215)
from the Newport Church Papers," which
looks very like a charge against Backus
of wilful deception.    And then he adds:

4*

"But one cannot help thinking that those 'Papers' must have been written long after the date of the occurrence . . . . and that their author confused the order of events." That those Papers are altogether trustworthy will be acknowledged when it is remembered that they were "gathered by the painstaking John Comer in 1726," and "were derived from Samuel Hubbard and Edward Smith, both members of the Newport Church, and contemporary with the events narrated." At any rate this testimony may be accepted as valid until some evidence to the contrary is presented more substantial than the unreasonable and preposterous conjectures of Dr. Palfrey and Dr. Dexter.

IX. Finally, the purpose of the visit to Mr. Witter, as thus declared and uniformly accepted to be the true one, is

entirely sufficient to account for it, and
harmonizes with all the circumstances.
Here was an old man far removed
from his brethren in the church, and
needing Christian sympathy and spiritual consolation, but by reason of age
and infirmity unable to make the long
journey to Newport. Dr. Dexter is
disposed to sneer at Witter's age and
inability to make the journey. But
Witter was within three years of three
score and ten. He is spoken of as being
disabled by infirmity such as "advanced
age" often brings with it, and moreover
as being blind. The journey from Lynn
to Newport, for such a man, in those
days, was no slight undertaking. It was
very suitable that the church should re-
member him in his loneliness and feeble-
ness, — surrounded by those who were
hostile to his faith, and probably soon

to die.   It is quite possible that Dr.
Clarke and his companions may have
thought that in visiting so remote a
place as Swampscott they would escape
all observation.   However that may
have been, they passed quietly through
Boston, and having timed their journey
so as to reach Witter's house on Saturday evening, there they lodged.   It was
a brave, loving, Christian deed, in which
can be traced no shrewd policy other
than the prompting of a Christlike
sympathy, and no defiant purpose other
than a courageous willingness to endure
perilous exposure in order to minister
to one of Christ's imprisoned and needy
disciples.

Dr. Clarke published in England a
truthful account of this visit and the
treatment which the visitors received—
to make known, as he said, "how that

spirit by which they [the Massachusetts
authorities] are led, would order the
whole World, if either brought under
them or should come in unto them."
And when Dr. Dexter says that Clarke
was careful to declare that one purpose
which he had in view in it all, was to
show how they would treat Rhode Island Baptists, were they to be annexed
to their colony, he makes an utterly unwarranted, and it is difficult not to say
a wilfully false, inference from Clarke's
language.    For the language was not
intended to apply at all to the visit and
its motive, but only to the published
account of the visit; and even then
contains no such meaning as Dr. Dexter interprets into it.    Dr. Clarke was
showing simply how he and his companions were treated, and how all who
differed religiously from the Massachu-

setts authorities, would be likely to be treated, if they should fall into their hands. We have here an illustration of how an unresisted bias may disqualify a historian for his high office, and how a weak theory may seek to bolster itself up by a fallacious deduction.

It will be necessary to consider more briefly the two remaining points, viz., the alleged criminal conduct of Mr. Witter's visitors, and the punishment which they received at the hands of the Bay magistrates.

Having arrived at Mr. Witter's on Saturday evening, they thought it best "to worship God in their own way on the Lord's day" in Witter's house. Dr. Clarke, in his narrative, thus describes the scene: "Finding, by sad experience, that the hour of temptation spoken of was coming upon all the World (in a more eminent way) to try them that are upon the Earth, I fell upon the consideration of that Word of Promise, made to those that keep the Word of his Patience, which present thoughts, while in conscience towards God and good will unto his Saints, I was imparting to my Companions in the house where I lodged, and to 4 or 5 Strangers that came in unexpected after I had begun, opening and proving what is meant by the hour of Temptation, what by the Word of his patience," &c.   But the presence of these heretics had been discovered.   The scent of heresy was marvelously acute.   The quiet service in that remote place was suddenly interrupted by the entrance of two constables with a warrant, signed by Robert Bridges, for the arrest of "certain erroneous persons, being strangers."   The warrant, of course, was issued

before the service was held; therefore
the only offence thus far of Dr. Clarke
and his companions was that they were
there. Their polite request to be allowed
to complete the service was impolitely
refused. They offered no resistance to
their arrest and were taken to the "ordinary" for safe-keeping. In the afternoon they were compelled, against their
protest, to go to the public. religious
service.* They manifested their disap-
proval by silently reading during the

---

*Dr. Clarke said : "If thou forcest us into your
assembly, then shall we be constrained to declare our-
selves that we cannot hold communion with them."
Their opposition to going to this public service, and
their discourteous conduct while there, are to be accounted for on the ground of that intense and narrow
conscientiousness which characterized the times. It
prevailed everywhere. Whatsoever was not of faith,
in their judgment, was sin. They could not even appear to fellowship and indorse it, or to show any
sympathy with it. Clarke and his companions could
not, in conscience, be present at this Sunday afternoon
service without giving expression to their disfellow-
ship and disapprobation.

service, and by failing to remove their
hats, which the constable removed for
them. When the service was over, Dr.
Clarke rose and said: "I desire as a
stranger, if I may, to propose a few
things to this Congregation, hoping, in
the proposall thereof, I shall commend
myself to your consciences to be guided
by that wisdom that is from above,
which, being pure, is also peaceable,
gentle, and easie to be intreated." He
was not allowed to proceed, and the
prisoners were remanded to the "ordinary." They were sent to prison in
Boston by the *mittimus* of Mr. Bridges
under date of Tuesday, July 22d.

The language of the *mittimus* is significant as disclosing the nature of their
offences, viz.: "for being at a Private
Meeting at Lin upon the Lord's day,
exercising upon themselves," "for of-

5

fensively disturbing the peace of the Congregation at their coming into the Publique Meeting," "for saying and manifesting that the church of Lin was not constituted according to the order of our Lord &c, for such other things as shall be alleged against them concerning their seducing and drawing aside of others after their erroneous judgments and practices, and for suspition of having their hands in the rebaptizing of one, or more, among us."

The magistrates, in the exercise of their judicial watchfulness against the awful sin of Anabaptism, *suspected* that there had been a baptism. Dr. Clarke was charged also with having administered the Lord's Supper while there. Such was the nature of their offences. It is not necessary to consider at this time whether the suspicions of the authorities were well-founded or not. The probability is that they were only suspicions.* But, in any event, there was no disturbance of the peace, no violation of any civil law,—only the exercise of the right to worship God in their own way, and gather comfort from his truth and ordinances within the sacred temple and castle of a man's private dwelling.

We now come to the concluding and most distressing part of this transaction, viz., the punishment which was inflicted upon these three offenders, and especially upon Mr. Holmes. Having been taken to Boston, they were arraigned the following week, on Thursday, July 31st. Dr. Clarke says: "In the forenoon we were examined; in the afternoon, without producing either accuser, witness,

---

* This question is fully considered in my "Early Baptists Defended," p. 32-37.

jury, law of God or man, we were sentenced." During the examination Governor Endicott charged them with being Anabaptists; to whom Clarke replied that he was "neither an Anabaptist, nor a Pedobaptist, nor a Catabaptist." The Governor lost his temper, and declared they "deserved death, and he would not have such trash brought into their jurisdiction"; also insinuating that they had influence over weak-minded persons only, and daring them to hold a discussion with the ministers. This challenge Dr. Clarke promptly accepted, and endeavored to bring about the desired discussion. The magistrates seemed at first to consent, but after some delay it came to naught. The excitement at the time of the so-called "trial" must have been intense,—not that it would take much "to put John Endi-

cott in a towering passion at any time."
But even John Wilson, the pastor, struck
and cursed Holmes, saying: "The curse
of God or Jesus goe with thee," because
Holmes had meekly said: "I blesse God
I am counted worthy to suffer for the
name of Jesus."

The sentences of the three men varied
in severity. Crandall was sentenced to
pay five pounds or to be well whipped,
Clarke to pay twenty pounds or to be
well whipped, and Holmes to pay
thirty pounds or to be well whipped.
Crandall's punishment was the lightest,
because he was the least prominent.
Holmes' was the heaviest undoubtedly
because he had been excommunicated
from the church at Rehoboth, and having been guilty of baptizing had been
dealt lightly with by the Court at Plymouth. Massachusetts sent a remon-

5*

strance at the time. They now had the
criminal in their own power, and felt
themselves called upon to make amends
for Plymouth's leniency, and to see that
justice was meted out. Criminals of
such a dangerous character must not
go unpunished. Not only his present
transgression but the sins of "other
times" were charged against him; and
now that he was in their jurisdiction
they would make him suffer for sins
committed out of their jurisdiction. So
reasoned these self-appointed guardians
of the new world's faith and peace, who
looked upon themselves as God's ministers of justice, — for their neighbors as
well as for themselves.

The fines imposed upon Crandall and
Clarke were paid by "tender-hearted
friends, without their consent and contrary to their judgment," though the

matter has an entirely different and untruthful aspect in the accounts of John Cotton and Dr. Dexter. Cotton, who justified the whole transaction, said Clarke "was contented to have his fine paid for him," and Dr. Dexter represents him, notwithstanding his alleged eagerness to suffer persecution according to his theory, as "very willing to leave for home."

There were those, too, who would have paid the fine of Holmes; but, to use his own words, he "durst not accept of deliverance in such a way." His conscience compelled him to refuse the friendly offer, lest he should appear to confess himself a transgressor.* It seems

---

* Cotton's letter to Sir Richard Saltonstall in defence of the Puritan magistrates is a remarkable document. In it he seeks to throw the responsibility of the whipping upon Holmes himself: "As for his whipping, it was more voluntarily chosen by him than inflicted on

certain from the narrative, not only that
he was unwilling to allow the fine to be
paid, but that, as he was the greatest
offender in the judgment of the authorities, they were not willing to allow it
to be paid, as they had been in the case
of the others. They made his case an
exception, and held him to the letter of

him. His censure by the Court was to have paid (as I
know) thirty pounds, or else be whipped ; his fine was
offered to be paid by friends for him freely, but he
chose rather to be whipped ; in which case, if his suffering of stripes was any worship of God at all, surely
it could be accounted no better than will-worship."
To which Governor Jenks replies : "Although the
paying of a fine seems to be but a small thing in
comparison of a man's parting with his religion, yet
the paying of a fine is the acknowledgment of a transgression ; and for a man to acknowledge that he has
transgressed, when his conscience tells him he has not,
is but little, if anything at all, short of parting with
his religion." Cotton seems to have been incapable of
understanding that there could be a great principle in-
volved in Holmes' unwillingness to consent to have his
fine paid, and sees in it, or pretends to see in it, only a
spirit of wilful obstinacy, which chose the whipping
rather than to be released.

the penalty,—inflicting upon him the cruel punishment of thirty stripes,— which was the penalty for the crimes of adultery, rape, and counterfeiting, and was, within ten stripes, the maximum number allowed by law.

The account of the cruel whipping is given in very touching Christian language in Holmes' letter to the brethren in London.  Having been kept in prison until September, he was led forth to his punishment, cheerfully trusting in God and in the righteousness of his cause, and taking his Testament in his hand as being the substance of his faith and the source of his comfort and strength. When he had been stripped of his clothing,—he neither assisting nor resisting, and telling them that for all Boston he would not give his body into their hands thus to be bruised upon any other account, yet upon this he would not give the hundredth part of a wampum peague (the sixth part of a penny) to free it out of their hands, and that he made as much conscience of unbuttoning one button as he did of paying the thirty pounds, — the executioner was commanded to "doe his office."

"As the man began to lay the stroaks upon my back," wrote the sufferer, "I said to the people, though my Flesh should fail and my Spirit should fail, yet God would not fail; so it pleased the Lord to come in and to so fill my heart and tongue as a vessel full, and with an audible voyce I brake forth, praying unto the Lord not to lay this Sin to their charge, and telling the people that now I found he did not fail me; and therefore, now I should

trust him forever who failed me not;
for in truth, as the stroaks fell upon
me, I had such a spirituall manifestation of God's presence, as the like thereunto I never had, nor felt, nor can with
fleshly tongue expresse; and the outward pain was so removed from me,
that indeed I am not able to declare it
to you; it was so easy to me that I
could well bear it, yea, and in a manner
felt it not, although it was grievous; as
the Spectators said, the Man striking
with all his strength (yea, spitting on
his hands three times, as many affirmed)
with a three-coarded whip, giving me
therewith thirty stroaks. When he had
loosed me from the Post, having joyfulnesse in my heart, and cheerfulness in
my countenance, as the Spectators observed, I told the Magistrates — You
have struck me as with Roses; and said

moreover Although the Lord hath made
it easie to me, yet I pray it may not be
laid to your charge."

Such is the plain, pathetic story of his
sufferings, as told by Holmes himself, in
which he sought to exalt the wonderful
grace of God which sustained him, and
manifested in a remarkable degree the
spirit of a Christlike forgiveness. So
severe was his punishment that the
hearts of the spectators were moved to
a sympathy which they could not repress, although the expression of it put
them in peril of like punishment. A
former acquaintance visited him, when
taken back to prison, and, as he said,
"poured oyl into my wound and plaistered my sores." That it was a cruel
punishment, inflicted with unmitigated
severity, no candid reader of the narrative will question for an instant.

Governor Joseph Jenks, writing in the
first third of the last century, so that
he must have received his information
from contemporaries of Holmes, describes it thus : " Mr. Holmes was
whipped thirty stripes, and in such an
unmerciful manner, that in many days,
if not some weeks, he could take no
rest but as he lay upon his knees and
elbows, not being able to suffer any
part of his body to touch the bed
whereon he lay." In similar language
Callender, Arnold, Oliver, Bancroft, Gay,
Adams, Straus and others describe the
whipping.

But Dr. Dexter in a remarkable note*
says : " Arnold thinks he was 'cruelly
whipped.' But Clarke says [he ought
to have inserted 'that Holmes said'] 
'It was so easie to me that I could well

*As to Roger Williams, p. 121.

6

bear it, and in a manner felt it not'; and that he told the magistrates after it was over 'You have struck me as with Roses.' Dr. Palfrey suspects the executioner had orders 'to vindicate what they thought the majesty of the law at little cost to the delinquent.'"

Dr. Dexter would have his readers understand that Holmes' punishment may not have been very severe, after all; that it may have been little more than a farce, an apparent vindication of the majesty of the law; and he throws back the responsibility of the insinuation upon his great master, Dr. Palfrey, who, he says, "suspects" that it may have been so. Having had our confidence in Dr. Dexter's fairness seriously shaken, we feel compelled to verify his quotations, even when he quotes from Dr. Palfrey. Turning to Palfrey's History, we read: "When he (Holmes) relates that the scourging which he endured 'was so easy to him that he could well bear it, yea, and in a manner felt it not, and that he told the Magistrates 'You have struck me as with Roses,' the reader ventures to hope that the executioner had been directed by his superiors to vindicate what they thought the majesty of the law, at little cost to the delinquent."

The phrase used is, it will be noticed, "the reader ventures to hope." To be sure, to ordinary readers such a hope is considerable of a venture, in the face of the facts as narrated, which both Dr. Palfrey and Dr. Dexter must have had before them. If it was only a humane "hope," it might be allowed to pass unnoticed. But the "hope" of Dr. Palfrey, unwarranted as that is, is magnified and

perverted into a "suspicion" in the pro-
cess of quotation by Dr. Dexter; and
when he seeks to ground that suspicion
upon the pathetic words of the patient
sufferer, and to ascribe the effect of the
sustaining grace of God to the imagined
grace of the executioner or the magistrates, he is guilty of a palpable, gross
and unpardonable misrepresentation.

Such a note as Dr. Dexter's, the intent of which is so manifestly uncandid,
and which presents a monstrous distor-
tion of the truth, is sufficient to destroy
confidence in any volume, or in the
honest purpose of the author to write
history fairly.

The Puritan magistrates were in no
mood to play a farce; they were in dead
earnest. They were bent on tragedy.
In their judgment Holmes was guilty
of a most serious crime. Governor En-

dicott had told him he deserved death,
and the meek pastor, John Wilson, had
"struck and cursed" the prisoner in holy
indignation, in "the exquisite rancor of
theological hatred." The executioner is
represented as "striking with all his
strength, yea, spitting on his hands
three times, as many affirmed." Warrants were issued for no less than thir-
teen persons who were unable to repress
their compassion for Holmes at the time
of the whipping. The most of them,
however, escaped. Two only, — John
Spur and John Hazel, who had taken
the bleeding sufferer by the hand as he
was led away from the whipping-post, —
were arrested ; and it is more than inti-
mated that there would have been more
whipping had not the executioner taken
himself out of the way so that he could
not be found. — having probably had

6*

enough of the bloody work. There is only one possible conclusion to be accepted, viz., that never was sentence of court executed more literally, never did executioner do his work more faithfully.

It has not been a pleasant duty to dwell upon these painful details. But the memories of men who were loyal to their convictions of truth and the rights of conscience, and to their more perfect views of soul-liberty, are as sacred as the memories of those who made them to suffer, and as worthy of being protected from sacrilegious assault. Better that this whole transaction should be passed by in silence — as it was by Captain Johnson in his "History of 1654," by Mr. Morton in his "New England Memorial of 1669," by Mr. Hubbard in his "History of 1680," by Cotton Mather in his "History of 1702," and by Gover-

nor Hutchinson in the first two volumes
of his History — than that, for the sake
of justifying the persecutors, the motives
of the persecuted should be maligned,
and their sufferings for the sake of conscience and liberty should be made light
of. John Clarke, the learned physician
and able pastor of the Newport Baptist
Church was in some respects the peer
of Roger Williams, though less widely
known and honored.*    Obadiah Holmes,

*Rev. John Callender says of Dr. Clarke : "He was
a faithful and useful minister, courteous in all the relations of life, and an ornament to his profession and to
the several offices which he sustained.  His memory is
deserving of lasting honor for his efforts toward establishing the first government in the world which gave
to all equal civil and religious liberty.  To no man is
Rhode Island more indebted than to him.  He was one
of the original projectors of the settlement of the Island, and one of its ablest legislators.  No character in
New England is of purer fame than John Clarke."  It
is not known where Dr. Clarke was educated ; but the
following item in his will shows him to have been a
man of wide learning and studious habits : "Unto my
loving friend, Richard Bayley, I give and bequeath my

the martyr of heavenly spirit and triumphant faith, was Dr. Clarke's honored
successor in the pastoral office for thirty
years.* The unchristian and inhuman
treatment of these worthies called forth
remonstrances on both sides of the At-
lantic. Sir Richard Saltonstall, one of
the first magistrates of the Massachu-

concordance and lexicon thereto belonging, written by
myself, being the fruit of several years' study, my
Hebrew Bible, Buxtorff's and Parsons' lexicons, Cotton's Concordance, and all the rest of my books." He
did not return from his mission to England till 1664,
having remained there as the agent of the Colony. He
died April 20, 1676.

*Obadiah Holmes was born at Preston, Lancashire,
England, about the year 1606, and came to this country
about 1639. He belonged to a family of considerable
means and of acknowledged respectability. He said of
his parents : "They were faithful in their generation,
and of good report among men, and brought up their
children tenderly and honorably." Three sons were
educated at Oxford, one of whom was probably Obadiah. This is evidence that the family was in ample
circumstances and of more than ordinary culture. Obadiah Holmes died in 1682, leaving a large posterity,
some of whom have obtained distinction in the learned
professions.

setts Bay, who was at the time in England, wrote sharply rebuking Cotton and Wilson for their "tyranny and persecution in New England as that you fine, whip and imprison men for their consciences. . . . . We pray for you and wish you prosperity every way; hoped the Lord would have given you so much light and love there, that you might have been eyes to God's people here, and not to practice those courses in a wilderness which you went so far to prevent." And Roger Williams—the great apostle of religious liberty, whose voice, from before his banishment until the day of his death, ceased not to proclaim the sublime principle of which his name will ever be the illustrious exponent—wrote to Governor Endicott such characteristic words as these: "Sir, I must be humbly bold to say 'tis impos-

sible for any man or men to maintain
their Christ by their sword, and to worship a true Christ! to fight against all
consciences opposite theirs, and not to
fight against God in some of them, and
to hunt after the precious life of the
Lord Jesus Christ."

The true philosophical historian cannot treat this incident, which we have
been considering, as an isolated phenom-
enon.   It was symptomatic of a social
condition and of a prevailing religious
spirit.   It reveals to us the attitude —
conscientious, indeed, but nevertheless
the attitude—of the ruling minds among
the Puritans.   It was not necessary for
a man to be a disturber of the peace in
order to be whipped or banished; or
rather, whoever differed from them in
religious faith or practice, and claimed
the right to indulge the exercise thereof,

was, in their judgment, a disturber of
the peace.   Uniformity of religious belief was the animating purpose of their
government, the sacred end of their legislation, a principal object of their social
compact and existence.   The language
of James I. expressed their sentiment
towards all dissentients : "I will make
them conform, or I will harry them out
of my kingdom."   There are men to-day
who boast of their descent from the
Puritans, and laud their excellencies—
and rightly so—who would not have
been allowed to remain within their borders twenty-four hours unmolested.

This incident throws its light upon that
long series of persecutions, in which the
Puritan magistrates solemnly delighted
themselves, of Church of England men,
Antinomians, Quakers, and Anabaptists.
This incident throws light—if any is

needed—upon the cause of the banishment of Roger Williams, which some-
what memorable event took place only
fifteen years before. The spirit of the
Puritan magistrates had suffered no
change in that interval of time. It was
neither better, nor worse, nor different.
They tried to be consistent, and to make
their principles of Church and State
triumphant, though no candid man is
now rash enough to say that those principles were right. Dr. George E. Ellis
has truly said: "Intolerance was a necessary condition of their enterprise. They
feared and hated religious liberty." In
parallel words Professor J. L. Diman
describes them as "intolerant of difference of opinion, regarding liberty of
conscience with equal fear and hate."
And so they feared and hated Roger
Williams, who not only entertained

broad and correct views of religious
liberty, but advocated them as oppor-
tunity offered itself.

To make a distinction between a
man's religious opinions and his disposition, whose only offending was that
it defended those opinions, is to make
a distinction without great difference.
The phrase "disturber of the peace"
did not then signify any such thing as
it means to-day. None of those offenders had been guilty of any overt acts
against civil laws, but only of violation
of religious laws which were incorporated into civil legislation. To hold
religious opinions different from those
of the magistrates and the body of the
people, and to be disposed to advocate
them, was to be wickedly contentious
and criminal according to their stand-
ards. Religious offenders were politi-

7

cal offenders. It is evident enough to
candid students of colonial history that
it was not Roger Williams' disposition,
in distinction from his religious views,
that caused his banishment, but the disposition of the Puritan magistrates.

They indulged in no such hair-split-
ting and specious methods. To them
Roger Williams represented views and
ideas of liberty which they "feared
and hated." He was already accused
of anabaptism. It is recorded that
Elder Brewster, in 1633 or 1634, prevailed with the church in Plymouth
to grant Williams' request for dismis-
sion, "fearing that he would run the
same course of rigid separation and
anabaptistry which Mr. John Smyth
at Amsterdam had done," and that at
Salem, where the church though warned
against him had received him, "in one

year's time he had filled that place with
principles of rigid separation and tending to anabaptism."

Anabaptism was the synonym of religious liberty. It had been before
Christendom as a distinct movement for
a hundred years,—in Switzerland and
Germany, in Holland, and in England.
Its first confession of faith, issued in
1527 at Schleithheim, a little town near
Schaffhausen, openly claimed and pro-
claimed religious liberty. In the Neth-
erlands, during all the fierce struggle
for civil liberty, these people, it is said,
" kept intact their ideas of religious
liberty." The confession of faith issued
by the Anabaptists in London in 1611
contained the enunciation of the same
great principle; and in all these lands
their fidelity cost them their lives.
Mark Pattison, in his biography of

John Milton, whose broad views of toleration are well known, says, that on that account "every Philistine leveled at him the contemptuous epithet of Anabaptist most freely." So thoroughly was anabaptism identified with religious liberty, that, if any man advocated a more generous toleration, this epithet was hurled at him, and not only in the old world, but in this new world as well.

Roger Williams was, if not already an Anabaptist, fast tending to it. The Puritan magistrates understood perfectly what he stood for, — if some of their modern misinterpreters do not. Arnold says: "To fasten upon Roger Williams the stigma of factious opposition to the government is to belie history, by an effort to vindicate bigotry and tyranny at the expense of truth." In the charge against Williams—under which he was tried, convicted and banished—the first item, which may be supposed to contain the gravamen of their accusation, is: "That the magistrate ought not to punish the breach of the first Table except when the civil peace is endangered." While announcing the doctrine of the separation of Church and State, instead of being "a disturber of the peace," he is represented as carefully guarding it. In a summary of the charges against him, prepared by Williams himself in 1644, occurs the following specification: "That the civil magistrate's power extends only to the bodies and goods and outward state of men." Governor Haynes was still living, and the most of the others also who had had a hand in the banishment; but no denial of this specification was ever made.

7*

Again in 1652, in the letter of Williams to Governor Endicott — already quoted — which was occasioned by the cruel treatment of these peaceable Rhode Island visitors, the writer says : " At present let it not be offensive in your eyes that I single out another, a fourth point, *a cause of my banishment also,* wherein I greatly fear one or two sad evils which have befallen your soul and conscience ; the point is that of the civil magistrate dealing in matters of *conscience* and *religion,* as also of *persecuting* and *hunting* any for matters merely *spiritual* or *religious.*" Notice the phrase " a cause of my banishment also," as determining the fact that the same spirit of religious persecution which whipped Holmes banished Williams.

Moreover, in order to remove all question or doubt, if any remain in the minds of any persons, as to the cause of Williams' banishment, and to establish conclusively the fact that it was a difference of religious opinion that made him obnoxious to the Puritan magistrates, and that it was religious persecution that drove him out into the wilderness, we may cite an Act passed by the Council of Massachusetts, March 31st, 1676, conditionally revoking the original act of banishment. It is only recently that attention has been called to this act. It was published by Massachusetts in 1859 in Vol. II. of the "Acts of the Commissioners of the United Colonies." It was discovered in the Massachusetts archives after the printing of the body of the volume, and placed in the Introduction, and so was not properly indexed. It reads as follows:

" Whereas, Mr. Roger Williams stands

at present under a sentence of Restraint
from coming into this colony, yet considering how readyly & freely at all
tymes he hath served the English Interest in this time of warre with the
Indians, and manifested his particular
respects to the authority of this Colony
in several services desired of him, and
further understanding how by the last
assault of the Indians upon Providence
his house is burned and himself in his
old age reduced to an uncomfortable
and disabled state—Out of compassion
to him in this condition the Council doe
Order and Declare that if the sayed Mr.
Williams shall see cause and desire it,
he shall have liberty to repayre into
any of our Towns for his security and
comfortable abode during these Public
Troubles, he behaving himself peaceably
and inoffensively and *not disseminating*

*and venting any of his different opinions in matters of religion* to the dissatisfaction of any."

Forty years had gone by. Some of the actors in 1636 had undoubtedly—like Williams—been spared to 1676. He had gone out of their borders, but not out of their knowledge or out of their necessity. Twice at least, by his friendly interposition with the Indians, he had probably saved the inhabitants of the Bay from annihilation. He had heaped coals of fire upon their heads. He had asked the privilege of simply crossing their territory on the way to England, and had been refused. He had been their neighbor, but was still "feared and hated." They kept him at arm's length, lest the pestilential principles which he advocated and fostered across the line should infect them.

John Winthrop, who had assented to
his banishment, had indeed shown a
disposition to recall him, and to "confer
upon him some mark of distinguished
favor for his services." But adverse
counsels long prevailed, until at length
touched to some slight appreciation of
his generous and self-sacrificing services
in their behalf, and to some slight sympathy for his age and supposed suffering
and poverty, but not to any marked
degree of penitence for their past conduct, they were prompted to revoke the
act of banishment, and to permit him to
return temporarily "during these public
troubles,"—still, however, remembering
the nature of his offence by adding this
significant condition, that he shall "not
disseminate and vent any of his different opinions in matters of religion."
Dr. Dexter, whose reputation as an ex-

plorer of colonial literature was very great, confessedly wrote his monograph "because of the limited acquaintance of some of the earliest historians with the facts," and because they did not go back to "the only original authorities." This act of revocation must have escaped this careful and boastfully thorough investigator,—or, perhaps we should come nearer the truth if we said, he seems to have escaped it. As a revocation it could not have amounted to much to Roger Williams, for we cannot conceive of him as accepting such liberty at the price of stifled convictions, and as surrendering the priceless principle for which he had once suffered the loss of all things. But this act of 1676 ought to settle all dispute as to the cause of the banishment of Roger Williams, and to settle it forever.

# APPENDIXES

# APPENDIX I

*Warrant for the arrest of Clarke, Holmes and Crandall.*

" By virtue hereof, you are required to go to the house of William Witter, and so to search from house to house, for certain erronious persons, being Strangers, and them to apprehend, and in safe custody to keep, and tomorrow morning by eight of the Clock to bring before me.

ROBERT BRIDGES."

*Copy of the Mittimus.*

" To the Keeper of the Prison at Boston,

By virtue hereof you are required to take into your custody from the Constable of Lin, or his Deputy, the bodies of John Clark, Obediah Holmes, and John Crandall, and them to keep, untill the next County Court to be held at Boston, that they may then and there answer to such complaints as may be alleged against them, for being taken by the Constable at a Private Meeting at Lin upon the Lords day, exercising among themselves, to whom divers of the Town repaired, and joyned with them, and that in the time of Publick exercise of the Worship of God ; as also for offensively disturbing the peace of the Congregation at their coming into the Publique Meeting in the time of Prayer in the afternoon, and for saying and manifesting that the Church of Lin was not constituted according to the order of our Lord, &c., for such other things as shall be alleged against them, concerning their seducing and drawing aside of others after their erroneous judgements and practices, and for suspition of having their hands in the re-baptizing of one, or more among us, as also for neglecting or refusing to give in sufficient security for their appearance at the said Court ; hereof fail not at your perill, 22. 5. 51.

ROB. BRIDGES."

*The sentence of Holmes, (the sentences of Clarke
and Crandall were drawn up in similar language, there being slight variations in the
accusations and the penalties.)*

"Forasmuch as you Obediah Holmes, being
come into this Jurisdiction about the 21 of
the 5th M. did meet at one William Witters
house at Lin, and did hear privately (and at
other times being an Excommunicate person
did take upon you to Preach and to Baptize)
upon the Lords day, and other dayes, and
being taken then by the Constable, and coming
afterwards to the Assembly at Lin, did in dis-
respect of the Ordinance of God and his
Worship, keep on your hat, the Pastor being
in Prayer, insomuch that you would not give
reverence in veiling your hat, till it was forced
off your head to the disturbance of the Congregation, and professing against the Insti-
tution of the Church, as not being according
to the Gospell of Jesus Christ, and that you
the said Obediah Holmes did upon the day
following meet again at the said Williams
Witters, in contempt of Authority, you being

8*

then in the custody of the Law, and did there receive the Sacrament, being Excommunicate, and you did Baptize such as were Baptized before, and thereby did necessarily deny the Baptism that was before administered to be Baptism, the Churches no Churches, and also other Ordinances, and Ministers, as if all were a Nullity; And also did deny the lawfullness of Baptizing of Infants, and all this tends to the dishonour of God, the despising the ordinances of God among us, the peace of the Churches, and seducing the Subjects of this Commonwealth from the truth of the Gospel of Jesus Christ, and perverting the strait waies of the Lord, the Court doth fine you 30 pounds to be paid, or sufficient sureties that the said sum shall be paid by the first day of the next Court of Assistants, or else to be well whipt, and that you shall remain in Prison till it be paid, or security given in for it.

By the Court,

ENCREASE NOWELL."

# APPENDIX II

*Extracts from the letter of Holmes to friends
in London, addressed—*

"Unto the well beloved Brethren, John
Spilsbury, William Kiffen, and the rest that
in London stand fast in that Faith, and con-
tinue to walk stedfastly in that Order of the
Gospell which was once delivered unto the
Saints by Jesus Christ. Obediah Holmes an
unworthy witness that Jesus is the Lord, and
of late a Prisoner for Jesus sake at Boston,
sendeth greeting." After giving an account
of his conversion, change of religious views
and arrest by the Plymouth court, in connection with two others, all of whom were
severely reprimanded and discharged without punishment, the letter continues—

"Not long after these troubles I came upon
occasion of businesse into the Colony of the

Mathatusets, with two other Brethren, as
Brother Clark, being one of the two, can in-
form you, where we three were apprehended,
carried to the prison at Boston, and so to the
Court, and were all sentenced; what they
laid to my charge, you may here read in my
sentence: Vpon the pronouncing of which I
went from the Bar, I exprest my self in these
words: I blesse God I am counted worthy to
suffer for the name of Jesus; whereupon
John Wilson (their Pastor as they call him)
strook me before the Judgement Seat, and
cursed me, saying, The Curse of God or
Jesus goe with thee; so we were carried to
the Prison, where not long after I was deprived of my two loving Friends; at whose
departure the Adversary stept in, took hold
on my Spirit, and troubled me for the space
of an hour, and then the Lord came in, and
sweetly releeved me, causing me to look to
himself, so was I stayed, and refreshed in the
thoughts of my God; and although during
the time of my Imprisonment, the Tempter
was busie, yet it pleased God so to stand at
my right hand, that the motions were but

sudden, and so vanished away; and although
there were that would have payd the money
if I would accept it, yet I durst not accept of
deliverance in such a way, and therefore my
answer to them was, that although I would
acknowledge their love to a cup of cold
Water, yet could I not thank them for their
money if they should pay it: so the Court
drew neer, and the night before I should
suffer according to my sentence, it pleased
God I rested and slept quietly; in the morning many Friends came to visit me, desiring
me to take the refreshment of Wine, and
other Comforts, but my resolution was not
to drink Wine, nor strong drink that day
untill my punishment were over, and the
reason was, lest in case I had more strength,
courage and boldnesse than ordinarily could
be expected, the VVorld should either say he
is drunk with new VVine, or else that the
comfort and strength of the Creature hath
carried him through, but my course was this:
I desired Brother John Hazell to bear my
Friends company, and I betook myself to my
Chamber, where I might communicate with

my God, commit myself to him, and beg
strength from him.

.  .      .        .    .

.  .  .  .  .  .  .  .  .  And when I
heard the voyce of my Keeper come for me,
even cheerfulnesse did come upon me, and
taking my Testament in my hand, I went
along with him to the place of execution, and
after common salutation there stood; there
stood by also one of the Magistrates, by
name Mr. Encrease Nowell, who for a while
kept silent, and spoke not a word, and so did
I, expecting the Governors presence, but he
came not.   But after a while Mr. Nowell bad
the Executioner doe his Office, then I desired
to speak a few words, but Mr. Nowell an-
swered, it is not now a time to speak, whereupon I took leave, [permission] and said,
Men, Brethren, Fathers, and Countrey-men,
I beseech you give me leave to speak a few
words, and the rather, because here are many
Spectators to see me punished, and I am to
seal with my Blood, if God give me strength,
that which I hold and practise in reference
to the Word of God, and the testimony of

Jesus; that which I have to say in brief is
this, Although I confesse I am no Disputant,
yet seeing I am to seal what I hold with my
Blood, I am ready to defend it by the Word,
and to dispute that point with any that shall
come forth to withstand it. Mr. Nowell an-
swered me, now was no time to dispute, then
said I, then I desire to give an account of the
Faith and Order I hold, and this I desired
three times, but in comes Mr. Flint, and saith
to the Executioner, Fellow, doe thine Office,
for this fellow would but make a long Speech
to delude the people.         .     .     .     .     .

.     .     .     .     .     .     . And in the time
of his pulling of my cloathes I continued
speaking, telling them, That I had so learned,
that for all Boston, I would not give my
bodie into their hands thus to be bruised
upon another account, yet upon this I would
not give the hundredth part of a *Wampon
Peague* to free it out of their hands, and that
I made as much Conscience of unbuttoning
one button, as I did of paying the 30l. in
reference thereunto; I told them moreover,
the Lord having manifested his love towards

me, in giving me repentance towards God,
and faith in Jesus Christ, and so to be baptized in water by a Messenger of Jesus into
the name of the Father, Son, and Holy Spirit,
wherein I have fellowship with him in his
death, buriall, and resurrection, I am now
come to be baptized in afflictions by your
hands, that so I may have further fellowship
with my Lord, and am not ashamed of his
sufferings, for by his stripes am I healed;
And as the man began to lay the stroaks
upon my back, I said to the people, though
my Flesh should fail, and my Spirit should
fail, yet God would not fail; so it pleased the
Lord to come in, and so to fill my heart and
tongue as a vessell full, and with an audible
voyce I broke forth, praying unto the Lord
not to lay this Sin to their charge, and telling the people, That now I found he did not
fail me, and therefore now I should trust him
forever who failed me not; for in truth, as
the stroaks fell upon me, I had such a spirituall manifestation of God's presence, as the
like thereunto I never had, nor felt, nor can
with fleshly tongue expresse, and the outward

pain was so removed from me, that indeed I
am not able to declare it to you, it was so easie
to me, that I could well bear it, yea and in a
manner felt it not, although it was grievous,
as the Spectators said, the Man striking with
all his strength (yea spitting on his hand
three times, as many affirmed) with a three-
coarded whip, giving me therewith thirty
stroaks; when he had loosed me from the
Post, having joyfulnesse in my heart, and
cheerfulnesse in my countenance, as the
Spectators observed, I told the Magistrates,
you have struck me as with Roses; and said
moreover, Although the Lord hath made it
easie to me, yet I pray God it may not be
laid to your charge. After this many came
to me, rejoycing to see the power of the Lord
manifested in weak flesh; but sinfull flesh
takes occasion hereby to bring others in
trouble, informs the Magistrates hereof, and
so two more are apprehended as for contempt
of authority, there names were John Hazell
and John Spur, who came indeed and did
shake me by the hand, but did use no words
of contempt or reproach unto any; no man

9

can prove that the first spoke any thing, and
for the second, he only said thus, Blessed be
the Lord ; yet these two for taking me by the
hand, and thus saying after I had received
my punishment, were sentenced to pay 40
shillings, or to be whipt. Both were resolved
against paying their Fine : Nevertheless after
one or two dayes imprisonment, one payed
John Spurs Fine, and he was released, and
after six or seven dayes Imprisonment of
Brother Hazell, even the day when he should
have suffered an other payed his, and so he
escaped, and the next day went to visit a
Friend about 6 miles from Boston, where he
the same day fell sick, and within 10 dayes
he ended this life ; when I was come to the
Prison, it pleased God to stir up the heart of
an old acquaintance of mine, who with much
tendernesse, like the good Samaritan, poured
oyl into my wound, and plaistered my sores ;
but there was present information given what
was done, and inquiry made who was the
Chirurgion, and it was commonly reported he
should be sent for, but what was done, I yet
know not. Now thus it hath pleased the

Father of Mercies so to dispose of the matter,
that my Bonds and Imprisonments have been
no hinderance to the Gospel, for before my
return, some submitted to the Lord, and were
baptized, and divers were put upon the way
of enquiry; And now being advised to make
my escape by night, because it was reported
that there were Warrants forth for me, I departed: and the next day after, while I was
on my Journey, the Constable came to search
at the house where I lodged, so I escaped
their hands, and was by the good hand of my
heavenly Father brought home again to my
neer relations, my wife, and eight children,
the Brethren of our Town and Providence
having taken pains to meet me 4 miles in the
woods, where we rejoyced together in the
Lord. Thus have I given you as briefly as I
can, a true relation of things: wherefore my
Brethren, rejoyce with me in the Lord, and
give all glory to him, for he is worthy, to
whom be praise for evermore, to whom I
commit you, and put up my earnest prayers
for you, that by my late experience, who
have trusted in God, and have not been de-

ceived, you may trust in him perfectly : wherefore my dearly beloved Brethren trust in the Lord, and you shall not be ashamed, nor confounded, so I also rest,

Yours in the bond of Charity,

OBEDIAH HOLMES."

# BIBLIOGRAPHY AND INDEX

9*

# BIBLIOGRAPHY

Acts of the Commissioners of the United Colonies, Vol. II.

Address at the Unveiling of the Statue of Roger Williams in Providence, by Prof. J. L. Diman.

Allen's Biographical Dictionary—(Sketch of John Clarke).

Annals of the Baptist Pulpit—(Sketch of John Clarke), by Wm. B. Sprague, D.D.

As to Roger Williams, by Henry M. Dexter, D.D.

Bancroft's History of the United States, Vols. I and II.

Baptist Quarterly, Vol. X. Article by C. E. Barrows, D.D.

Bryant's Popular History of the United States, Vol. II, by William C. Bryant and Sidney H. Gay.

**Historical Discourse,** by Rev. John Callender.

**History of the Baptists, Vol. I,** by Isaac Backus.

**History of the Baptists,** by Thomas Armitage, D.D.

**History of the Baptists in New England,** by Henry S. Burrage, D.D.

**History of the Baptists in the United States,** by Prof. Albert H. Newman, D.D.

**History of Lynn,** by Alonzo Lewis.

**History of Lynn,** by Lewis and Newhall.

**History of New England, Vol. II,** by John G. Palfrey, D.D., LL.D.

**History of Massachusetts, First Period,** by J. L. Barry.

**History of Rhode Island, Vol. I,** by Samuel Greene Arnold.

**Hubbard's History of New England.**

Hutchinson's History of Massachusetts.

Hutchinson's Collection of Original Papers.

Life of Roger Williams, in Sparks' Am. Biography, New Series, Vol. IV, by Prof. William Gammell.

Life of Roger Williams, by Romeo Elton, D.D.

Massachusetts Archives, Vol. II.

Massachusetts Historical Collections, Vol. II, Fourth Series.

Massachusetts, Its Historians and Its History, by Charles Francis Adams.

Massachusetts Records, Vol. III.

Memoir of Roger Williams, by Prof. James D. Knowles.

Morton's Memorial.

Neal's History of New England.

Newport Church Papers, compiled by Rev. John Comer.

Plymouth Records, Vol. II.

Puritan Commonwealth, by Peter Oliver.

Rhode Island Colonial Records, Vol. I.

Roger Williams, the Pioneer of Religious Liberty, by Oscar S. Straus.

Savage's Genealogical Dictionary, Vol. IV—(Sketch of William Witter).

Short History of the Baptists, by Prof. Henry C. Vedder.

The Emancipation of Massachusetts, by Brooks Adams.

Winthrop's Journal, Vol. II.

# INDEX

## A.

**Adams,** Brooks, 61.

**Anabaptism,** charge of, against The Three Rhode Islanders, 50, 52 ; charge of, against Roger Williams, 74 ; meaning of, 75, 76 ; confession of faith of, (1611), 75.

**Anabaptists,** 27 ; persecutions of, 71.

**Antinomians,** 71.

**Arnold's** "History of Rhode Island" : as to the visit, 12 ; as to whipping of Holmes, 61 ; as to Roger Williams, 76.

## B.

**Backus'** "History of the Baptists," 11, 41.

**Bancroft's** "History of the United States" : as to the character of Clarke, 24 ; as to whipping of Holmes, 61.

**Baptism,** Infant : Witter's opinion of, 12 ; law of 1644 concerning, 20, 34.

**Baptists,** hostility to, by Massachusetts, 19, 21, 33, 38, 45.

10

## D.

**Dexter,** Dr. H. M. : author of " As to Roger Williams," 8 ; disciple of Dr. Palfrey, 25 ; his account of the visit to Witter, 26 ; errors of his view, 28–32 ; throws discredit on Newport Church Papers, 41, 42 ; view of, on Witter's age, 43 ; his interpretation of Clarke's own statement as to object of the visit, 45 ; his interpretation of payment of Clarke's fine, 55 ; his account of Holmes' whipping, 61 ; as an historical authority, 64 ; failure of, to see act of revocation of Roger Williams, 83 ; criticism of, 64–66.

**Diman,** J. L., 72.

**"Disturber** of the peace " : meaning of, 70, 73, 77.

## E.

**Easton,** Nicholas, 39.

**Ellis,** Dr. Geo. E., 72.

**Endicott,** Gov. John : at trial of the three Rhode Islanders, 52, 58, 64, 65 ; letter to, from Roger Williams concerning punishment of Clarke, 69, 78.

## G.

**Gay,** Sidney H., 61.

## H.

**Haynes,** Gov., 77.

## M.

## N.

## P.

## Q.

Quakers, 71.

## R.

Rehoboth, 53.

Rhode Island : separate government of, established, 18 ; Coddington, governor of, 26 ; unsettled condition of, 26 ; as to proposed introduction of, into Colonial Confederacy, 29 ; introduction of, not purpose of Coddington, 32, 36, 37 ; separated from Providence and Warwick, 37 ; intolerable to Boston, 38.

Rhode Island Plantations, 26.

## S.

Salem : Church of, 74.

Saltonstall, Sir Richard : Cotton's letter to, 55 (foot note) ; opinion of, on punishment of Holmes 68, 69.

Schleithheim : confession of faith issued at, 75.

Smith, Edward, 42.

Smyth, John, 74.

Spilsbury, John, 13, 91.

Spur, John, 65, 97, 98.

Straus, Oscar S., 61.

# W.

# PUBLICATIONS

OF

# PRESTON & ROUNDS,

PROVIDENCE, R.I.

# History of the State of Rhode Island and Providence Plantations, 1636-1790.

## By SAMUEL GREENE ARNOLD.

New Edition. 2 vols. Octavo. 574 and 600 pp. $7.50, net.

---

Governor Arnold's History of Rhode Island, based upon a careful study of documents in the British State Paper Office and in the Rhode Island State Archives, supplemented by investigations at Paris and The Hague, has from its publication been the authoritative history of the State.

Genealogical students will find in these volumes the names of over fifteen hundred persons prominent in Rhode Island affairs. This work is of much more than local interest, as the experiment of religious liberty here tried gives to this history an importance far beyond the narrow limits of the State.

---

" One of the best State histories ever written is S. G. Arnold's History of the State of Rhode Island and Providence Plantations." — JOHN FISKE.

" The best history of Rhode Island is that of Arnold." — PROF. GEORGE P. FISHER, Yale University.

" Mr. Samuel Greene Arnold in his history of Rhode Island has brought together all the extant materials. He brings out more clearly than any previous writer the distinct threads of the previous settlements." PROF. JOHN A. DOYLE, Oxford.

" A work prepared after long and careful research. Probably no student has ever made himself more familiar with the history of Rhode Island than did Arnold. This work abounds, therefore, in valuable information." — PRES. CHARLES KENDALL ADAMS, Cornell University.

---

SENT POSTPAID BY THE PUBLISHERS.

# Among Rhode Island Wild Flowers.

By W. WHITMAN BAILEY,

*Professor of Botany, Brown University.*

Cloth.   16mo.   Three full-page Illustrations.   75 cents, net.

---

This admirable little volume, the outgrowth of the author's ripe experience in teaching and in botanizing, contains a popular and interesting account of Rhode Island wild flowers as distributed throughout the State.   The favorite collecting grounds are fully described, thus forming a botanical guide to Rhode Island.

In writing this volume Professor Bailey has had in mind the needs of the nature lover, and has discarded technical terms as far as possible, adapting the work to the amateur as well as the botanist.

It should be in the hands of every lover of woodland and meadow.

Forwarded postpaid to any address upon receipt of price by the publishers. .

# Tax Lists of the Town of Providence

### During the Administration of Sir Edmund Andros and his Council,

## 1686–1689.

### Compiled by EDWARD FIELD, A.B.,

*Member of the Rhode Island Historical Society, and one of the Record Commissioners of the City of Providence.*

### Cloth. Octavo. 60 pp. $1.00, net.

---

The "Tax Lists of the Town of Providence" is a compilation of original documents relating to taxation during the Administration of **Sir Edmund Andros and his Council, 1686-1689.** It comprises copies of warrants issued by order of the Council for the assessment and collection of taxes, the tax lists or rate bills prepared pursuant to these warrants, the returns made by the townsmen of their ratable property, and the Tax Laws enacted by Andros and his Council. All of these, with the exception of the laws, are here printed for the first time.

Among the rate bills is the list of polls for 1688, which contains the *names of all males sixteen years of age and upwards living in Providence in August of that year;* practically a census of the town. For the genealogist and historian this volume contains material of the greatest value on account of the great number of names which these lists contain, besides showing the amount of the tax assessment in each case.

The returns of ratable property form a study by themselves, for they tell in the quaint language of the colonists what they possess, and therefore shed much light on the condition of the times. For a study of this episode in New England Colonial History this work is invaluable.

The index of all names contained in the lists and text is a feature of this work.

The edition is limited to **two hundred and fifty** numbered copies.

Sent postpaid to any address on receipt of one dollar.

5

# Early Rhode Island Houses.

An Historical and Architectural Study by NORMAN M. ISHAM, Instructor in Architecture, Brown University, and ALBERT F. BROWN, Architect. Illustrated with a map and over fifty full-page plates. $3.50, net.

No feature in the study of the early life of New England is more valuable or more interesting than the architecture. Nothing throws more light on the home life of the colonists than the knowledge of how they planned and built their dwellings.

**Early Rhode Island Houses** gives a clear and accurate account of the early buildings and methods of construction, showing the historical development of architecture among the Rhode Island colonists, the striking individuality in the work of the colony and the wide difference between the buildings here and the contemporary dwelling in Massachusetts and Connecticut.

Those interested in colonial life may here look into the early homes of Rhode Island with their cavernous fireplaces and enormous beams. The student will find in these old examples a valuable commentary on New England history, while the architect will discover in the measurements and analyses of construction much of professional interest.

Among the houses described are the Smith Garrison House and the homesteads of the families of Fenner, Olney, Field, Crawford, Waterman, Mowry, Arnold, Whipple, and Manton.

A chapter is devoted to the early houses of Newport, which were unlike those of the northern part of the State and resemble the old work in the Hartford colony.

Photographs and measurements of the dwellings have been made, and from them careful plans, sections, and restorations have been drawn; in some cases six full-page plates admirably drawn and interesting in themselves have been devoted to a single house. Several large plates give illustrations of framing and other details. It is to be noted that these plates are made from measured drawings, that the measurements are given on the plates, and that these constitute in most if not all cases the only exact records for a class of buildings which is destined to disappear at no distant day. It is believed that these drawings, and especially the restorations, will give a clearer idea than has ever before been obtained of the early New England house. A map enables the reader to locate without difficulty the houses mentioned in the text.

The authors have discussed the historical relation of Rhode Island work to contemporary building in the other New England colonies and in the mother country. The book is a mine of authentic information on this subject.

A list of the houses in the State built before 1725, so far as they are known, with dates and a brief description will be found in the appendix.

"This book is probably the most valuable historic architectural treatise that has as yet appeared in America " — *The Nation.*

# Revolutionary Defences in Rhode Island.

An Historical Account of the Forts and Beacons erected during
the American Revolution.

## By EDWARD FIELD, A.B.,

*Past President of the Rhode Island Society of the
Sons of the American Revolution.*

NEARLY READY.

--- -- --- ---

# Rhode Island's Adoption of the Federal Constitution.

A Discourse before the Rhode Island Historical Society, at its
Centennial Celebration of Rhode Island's Adoption
of the Federal Constitution.

## By HORATIO ROGERS,

*President of the Society.*

**Paper. 44 pp. 8vo. 35 cents, net.**

This statement of the reasons which impelled the
state first to hesitate with anxious deliberation, and
afterwards freely and fully to abandon its independent
character, and become an integral part of an indissolu-
ble nation, is made in such form that it should be the
end of controversy, and the future student of history
should require no further material for a just and dis-
criminating conclusion.

# MARY DYER

Of Rhode Island, The Quaker Martyr that was
Hanged on Boston Common, June 1, 1660.

---

By HORATIO ROGERS, Associate Justice
of the Supreme Court of Rhode Island.

---

The author has gathered from many sources the scattered facts relating to the career of Mary Dyer and woven them into a detailed narrative, so that the tragic story of her life is now for the first time adequately told. By adding a brief but comprehensive sketch of the manner and sentiments of her times, he has furnished a background or framework for his subject which adds much to the interest of the volume by enabling the reader, the better to understand the surroundings of the characters he portrays. The important documents relating to her trial are printed in the appendix.

Cloth, 12mo., 115 pages. Price $1.00 net. Sent postpaid upon receipt of the price by the publishers.

# THE EAST INDIA TRADE

## OF PROVIDENCE,

### From 1787 to 1807.

### BY GERTRUDE SELWYN KIMBALL.

By a careful study of log books and commercial papers of the old shipping firms, the author is enabled to present an interesting picture of the East India Trade of Providence in its palmy days.

8vo. 34 pages, paper, 50 cents net.

Sent postpaid on receipt of price.

# THE MAGAZINE

....OF....

# NEW ENGLAND HISTORY.

## FOR 1891, 1892, 1893.

— -

Having purchased the few remaining complete sets of the Magazine of New England History, originally published at $5.00, we offer the three volumes in parts as issued for $2 50 net per set or bound in one volume, cloth, for $3.50 net.

These volumes contain nearly eight hundred pages of information relating to New England local, church and family history, including records, genealogies, journals, letters and many interesting notes and queries.

—

# WHAT CHEER

—OR—

## ROGER WILLIAMS IN BANISHMENT.

A Poem by JOB DURFEE.

Revised and edited by THOMAS DURFEE.

Cloth, Leather Label, 12 mo., 225 pages.   PRICE $1.25 NET

# TOPOGRAPHICAL ATLAS

OF THE

## STATE OF RHODE ISLAND AND PROVIDENCE PLANTATIONS.

—

## By the United States Geological Survey, in co-operation with the State.

———

Having secured the remaining copies of this Atlas we offer them at the following reduced prices.

| | |
|---|---|
| In sheets, | $1.00 |
| In portfolio, | 2.00 |
| Bound in cloth, | 2.50 |

A few bound in half morocco remain and can be furnished for $3.50.

The plates of this Atlas were engraved upon copper in the highest style of cartographic engraving by the United States Government and furnished to the State. From these plates transfers were made to stone and the maps printed in four colors, viz: The names, roads, railroads and other culture features are in *black*. Rivers, ponds, swamps and other water features are in *blue*. Contour lines and figures denoting elevation are in *brown*. State, county and town boundaries are in *pink* over the more exact boundaries in black or blue.

Besides showing all bodies of water and water courses, common roads or highways and railroads, it has one feature distinct from and superior to any map of the State hitherto published, viz: Contour lines, drawn for each 20 feet of elevation above mean sea level. Figures are placed upon the heavier contour lines which denote elevations of 100 feet, 200 feet, etc., above mean sea level, also upon hills and bodies of water to denote their elevation. A contour line indicating 20 feet depth of water *below* mean sea level is drawn along the coast. In a few cases figures are given to indicate depths of water of less than 20 feet.

This Atlas includes 12 maps and 10 pages index and statistics in all 22 sheets 21x16½. The scale of the survey is $\frac{1}{62500}$ or one mile to an inch.